Pick-A-Path™ #12

The Ballerina MYSTERY

by JAMIE PASCAL and LAURIE PASCAL
illustrated by JEAN JENKINS

SCHOLASTIC INC.
New York Toronto London Auckland Sydney Tokyo

ISBN 0-590-33048-9

12 11 10 9 8 7 6 5 4 3 2 4 5 6 7 8 9/8

Printed in the U.S.A. 11

For the best mother in the whole world, ours—
Francine Pascal

Scholastic Books in the Pick-A-Path Series

How many have you read?

#1 **THE DANDEE DIAMOND MYSTERY**
by Jane O'Connor and Joyce Milton

#2 **THE ROLLER COASTER GHOST**
by Fran Manushkin

#3 **THE GREAT BASEBALL CHAMPIONSHIP**
by Richard Wenk

#4 **THE AMAZING BUBBLEGUM CAPER**
by Jane O'Connor and Joyce Milton

#5 **THE SUPER TRAIL BIKE RACE**
by Richard Wenk

#6 **MYSTERY AT MOCKINGBIRD MANOR**
by Laurie Pascal and Jamie Pascal

#7 **THE FANTASTIC JOURNEY OF THE SPACE SHUTTLE *ASTRA***
by B. B. Hiller

#8 **THE MAGIC TOP MYSTERY**
by Jane O'Connor

#9 **JUNGLE ADVENTURE**
by Nora Logan

#10 **THE MYSTERY OF THE MISSING MUMMY**
by Kate McMullan

#11 **DINOSAUR ADVENTURE**
by Nora Logan

#12 **THE BALLERINA MYSTERY**
by Jamie Pascal and Laurie Pascal

READ THIS FIRST

Are you ready for some really fantastic adventures?

Start reading on page 1 and keep going until you have to make a choice. Then decide what you want to do and turn to that page.

Keep going until you reach **THE END**. Then, you can go back and start again. Every path leads to a new story!

It is all up to you!

KARAKOV
SCHOOL
OF
BALLET
STUDIO A

You have been studying ballet with Madame Karakov for two years. Every Saturday morning, you take the subway from your house into the city for your lesson. You don't mind waking up early, because you really love dancing.

You don't love Madame Karakov, though, because she can be pretty awful. Especially when she raps that stick on the floor just because your *plié* isn't perfect or your *arabesque* doesn't touch the ceiling. And if you accidentally whisper or giggle even the tiniest bit — forget it, she goes bananas in Russian, French, and almost English at the same time! Try to stop giggling when *that* happens.

Turn to **page 2.**

Still, you think dancing is fabulous, and when you grow up you're going to be a star ballerina for sure. Everyone says so — your mother, your father, and both your aunts. Harold, your older brother, doesn't know anything anyhow, so what he says doesn't count.

But you might not even have to wait until you grow up for your dream to come true. This year the National Ballet Company is going to choose one young ballerina to play the fairy princess in a new ballet. The ballerina will travel all over the U.S., dancing with the company. The grand finale will be a show at the White House.

You and your best friend in the whole world, Amy Webster, and your worst enemy, Gretta Gambol, have made it to the finals. You and Amy are very excited, but you wish Gretta wasn't also one of the finalists. There's usually some kind of trouble when she's around. Not just for you — for everyone.

Go on to the next page.

You have one month to prepare for the contest. The biggest name in the ballet world, Rudolf Rudemsky, will be one of the judges.

Today all the finalists have to be at Town Hall Dance Studio at three o'clock sharp to begin their lessons. You will all be learning the fairy princess's part to audition in the contest.

Amy and her mother are picking you up in twenty minutes, so you pack your ballet bag and are waiting to go when the phone rings. You answer it and a familiar voice says, "I'm sorry to tell you, but there's been a big mistake. You are *not* one of the finalists. Please don't go to the special lessons today."

If you think this call sounds fishy, turn to **page 33.**

If you throw yourself on your bed and cry, turn to **page 4.**

Not a finalist after all! You can hardly believe it. At least today is Friday and you won't have to face anyone till Monday.

You mope around the house all weekend. You are so unhappy and embarrassed you won't even talk to Amy. She's called five times.

Now it's Sunday evening. You've cried enough for a lifetime. Amy calls again, and this time you answer the phone because you don't want her to think you're angry at her. You tell her you were disqualified.

Go on to the next page.

"No, you weren't," she says. "Madame has been calling your name at every class, and she keeps asking where you are."

You tell Amy about the phone call and how you thought the voice sounded like someone you know. You both decide it must have been a *phony* phone call.

"But who would do such a terrible thing?" Amy asks.

And then it hits you. That was Gretta Gambol's voice!

If you decide to go to ballet class even though you've missed three lessons, turn to **page 6.**

If you decide to report Gretta to the National Ballet Company, turn to **page 32.**

Madame Karakov welcomes you into the special class, even though you've missed some lessons. "But you must work *extra* hard," she adds with a frown.

You work day and night, and you catch up so quickly that even Madame is surprised. She announces to the whole class how pleased she is.

Gretta is so jealous that she forgets some steps and bumps into the girl behind her. Madame Karakov shouts at Gretta in front of everyone. If they only knew what Gretta tried to do to you!

You keep on practicing every afternoon, and finally the big day arrives. You have the beautiful new tutu that your grandmother made you, your black satin ballet slippers, your gorgeous new pink satin toe — uh oh, trouble. Where are your toe shoes? You look everywhere, but you can't find them. Help!!!

Your pesky brother Harold must have hidden them like he did last week!

Turn to **page 7.**

You run to Harold's room and hear the TV through the door. Harold is always watching TV. This time his door is locked. You knock. No answer. You knock again.

"What d'ya want?" he growls.

"Did you take my toe shoes again?" you ask as nicely as you can.

"Uh-uh," he answers.

You don't believe him. "I know you did," you say.

"Did not," he says.

"Did too."

"Did not."

This could go on forever and you only have fifteen minutes. You tell him to open the door. He pretends he can't hear you.

If you run screaming to your mother,
turn to **page 16.**

If you try to trick him into
opening the door,
turn to **page 8.**

You stand outside Harold's door and scream at the top of your lungs. "If you don't open that door, you're going to be in big trouble when Mommy comes home."

Nice try, but he's too smart for that.

Then the phone rings. You race to answer it, hoping it's your mother. But it's the wrong number.

How can you get Harold to open that door? Suddenly you have an idea. Harold doesn't know it was a wrong number.

Go on to the next page.

"Haarrold," you call out in a singsongy voice. "Alice is on the phone."

Harold has been in love with Alice since the first day of school. As soon as you say her name, he flies out the door, still dressed in his muddy football uniform. The trick worked!

Turn to **page 10.**

You sneak into Harold's room and start to search. You rummage through a mountain of clothes so big it will take you till Christmas to find anything in there.

You are just about to give up when you spot a pink ribbon on the floor. It's got to be from your toe shoes! But where are they?

You look under the bed, in his dresser drawers, behind the desk — everywhere. The only place you haven't looked is in his closet. You open the door to look when suddenly Harold shoves you inside and slams the door.

Turn to **page 11.**

"Let me out of here or I'll clobber you!" you scream.

"No way," replies Harold. "You tricked me, and now you're gonna pay."

You hear Harold leave the room. You can't believe it. He's really going to leave you locked in.

You're about to give up all hope when you remember how Nancy Drew escaped from a locked closet. You take one of the wire coat-hangers, twist it until the top opens, and you have a genuine lock-picker.

In no time you have the door open. You check your watch. If you find your shoes, you can still make it to the contest. Maybe Harold hid them downstairs with the laundry. On the other hand, they might be in the garbage.

If you decide to look in the garbage, turn to **page 45.**

If you decide to search in the laundry room, turn to **page 13.**

You turn around and walk out of the building. You'll call up and apologize later. But you're just too frightened of that woman to stay for tea. Suddenly, two men dressed in dark suits are standing on either side of you.

"Don't say a word or there's going to be trouble," one of them says. You freeze in your tracks.

They shove you into a big black limousine with very dark windows so no one can see inside.

"We've got her," they say to the driver in an accent you can hardly understand.

Turn to **page 58.**

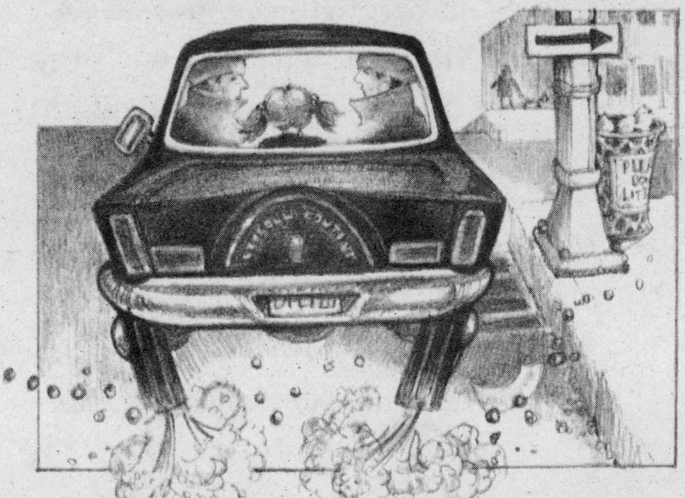

You fly down the hall as fast as you can. As you pass the laundry chute, something catches your eye. A pink ribbon! You were right. Harold must have thrown the shoes down the chute so he wouldn't get caught with the evidence. You've got to hurry. It's getting later and later.

You jump down the last two basement steps and start sorting through a whole pile of laundry — socks, sheets, towels — but the shoes aren't there. Maybe they got stuck in the laundry chute.

You get out the stepladder and try to push yourself up into the chute. It's very dark up there, but you feel sure that's where Harold stashed your shoes. You're on tiptoes now and the ladder is wobbling. There, you see them! Two pink shoes are sticking out from a rolled-up towel that is stuck in the chute. You reach up. The ladder is really shaking now. The shoes are still beyond your reach. You try once more. No luck.

Turn to **page 15.**

The ladder wobbles one more time and you fall onto the pile of laundry. You're sitting there — sadder than you ever remember. Just then Harold opens the chute upstairs and dumps in his old muddy football uniform. The weight of it pushes the towel and the shoes down the chute and right into your lap. Shoes in hand, you race outside. Your mother has just pulled into the driveway. She honks once and you jump into the car. Before you know it, you're at Town Hall and they're calling your name.

You dance your heart out. In spite of everything that happened, you know you've given the most fabulous performance of your life. Now all you can do is wait for the decision. . . .

THE END

"Mom!" you shout. "Harold won't give me my toe shoes!"

Your mother comes right away and makes him open the door. You search his room, but you can't find the shoes. Harold thinks it's all very funny. You'd like to bop him on the head, but you don't have the time. Besides, your mother is watching.

You can hear Amy's mother honking the horn outside. Now everyone begins to look for your toe shoes, even horrible Harold and your baby sister, Liza. And nobody can find them.

Mrs. Webster can't wait any longer. You're either going to have to go without your toe shoes or keep searching and miss the ride.

You decide to take your chances without your toe shoes.

Go on to the next page.

You get in the car, but you hardly say a word to Amy all the way to Town Hall. You know if you open your mouth you're going to cry. All you can think about is how horrible you feel. After all that practicing and hoping and wishing, you don't even have one tiny chance, because the toe dancing is the most important part of the audition.

Then suddenly, right out of the blue, you remember where you put your shoes.

"Amy! They're in the hall closet! Yesterday when I came home from school, instead of taking them up to my room, I threw them in the closet with my books. Maybe there's still a chance."

Maybe. . . .

If you phone your mother the minute you get to Town Hall, turn to **page 18.**

If you think you can make it home on the subway and be back in time for the audition, turn to **page 29.**

Inside the hall, everywhere you look there are ballerinas. You squeeze through the crowd, looking for a phone — you've got to call your mother right away. Oh, no! All the phones are taken.

Time is running out. At last someone hangs up, and you pop in your dime and dial. You tell your mother where the shoes are and she finds them right away. Fantastic!

"Oh, dear," she says, "Daddy is still out with the car."

Your stomach sinks.

"But I expect him home any minute, and just as soon as he gets here, we'll rush right over. Keep your fingers crossed," she says and hangs up.

You even cross your toes.

Turn to **page 20.**

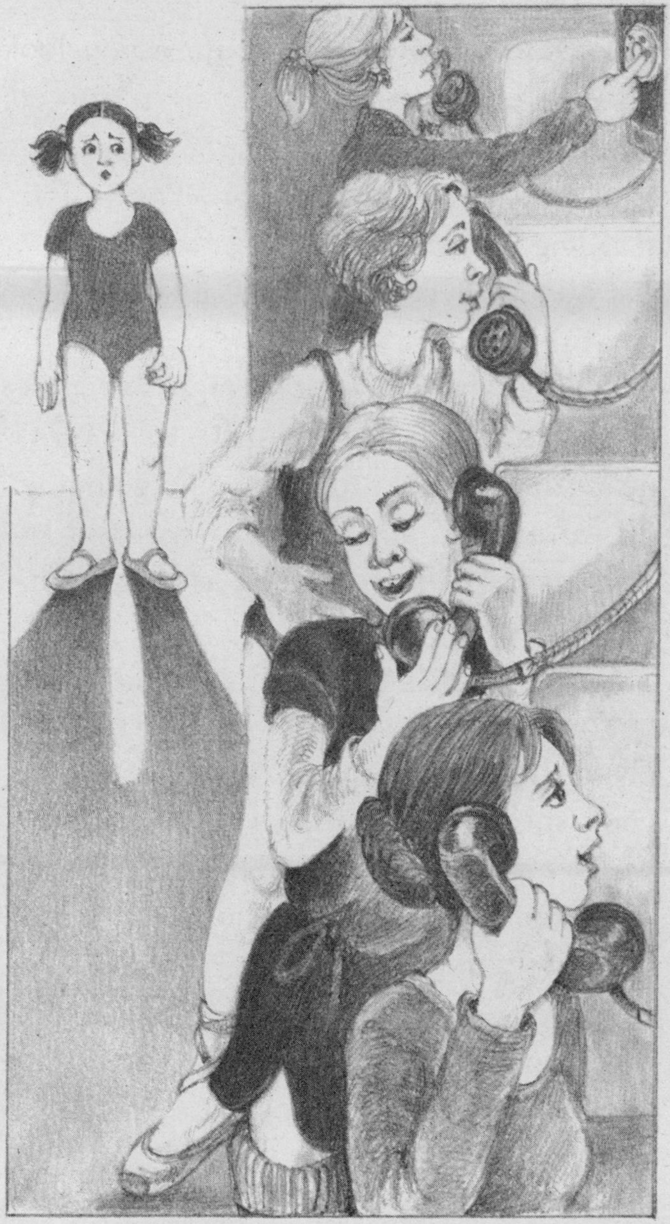

Amy agrees to go first to give you a little extra time.

"Next," the stage manager calls out, and Amy steps out on stage. You're left standing backstage with Gretta. She's the star of your ballet classes — at least that's what she thinks.

"If I were you," Gretta says, "I wouldn't even bother with the audition. You'll never do it without toe shoes. I'd go home if I were you."

"I may as well give it a try as long as I'm here," you say.

Gretta shrugs and turns away.

You watch Amy dance. She's very good. Even though she's your best friend, you wish she weren't quite so terrific. You wonder if you'd be as good even if you had your toe shoes. You make up your mind absolutely not to cry.

"Next."

It's your turn.

Go on to the next page.

The music starts, but it sounds very different than it did in class. There's a real orchestra playing down there. Wow, are your knees trembling.

"Okay, we're ready," one of the judges calls to you.

You walk onto the stage. Everything is dark in front of the footlights. You can't see the judges, but you sure know they're out there.

You move toward center stage, keeping your shoulders back, your head held high, and even remembering to tilt your chin ever so slightly. Holding your arms out, you begin your first twirl.

Turn to **page 22.**

Something magical begins to happen. You feel yourself twirling right into the music and letting it carry you up, up into the highest leaps you've ever reached. You're spinning faster than you've ever spun.

You know you've never felt this way before, never danced like this before. You feel like a real ballerina, and it's beautiful. But it's sad because you know you can't win.

The music ends and there is silence in the theater.

Turn to **page 24.**

"That was lovely," a voice from the dark says, "but you were supposed to dance in toe shoes. I'm sorry."

You turn around so they can't see your tears and make your way off the stage.

"Wait!" It's your mother, out of breath and running down the aisle, waving your beautiful pink toe shoes.

"All right," the voice from the dark calls out, "this time let's try it *en pointe.*"

The orchestra starts and you begin to dance. You get that warm, special feeling again, but this time it's even stronger. You want to dance forever.

Then the last note is being played and you're making a grand, sweeping curtsy and leaving the stage.

You were the last contestant. Now the judges must make their decision.

If you think you were the best,
turn to **page 27.**

If you think you were very good but
maybe Amy was a little better,
turn to **page 50.**

You dial 911 and tell the police what happened. All those spy and mystery books you read came in mighty handy. It occurred to you to memorize the license number of the car as it zoomed away. This turns out to be the most important information you can give the police.

On the way home in the police car you hear over the radio that the spies have been caught. Thank goodness!! Natasha is safe now.

You can both be in the contest. You wonder who will win. . . .

THE END

You just can't believe that Gretta can be so mean. How does she find the time? But you don't have the time to think about that now.

You search through your ballet bag and find four safety pins. Now all you need is some ribbon. You look around. Nothing. Tears well up in your eyes. You plop yourself down on the floor, almost ready to give up. As you're sitting there, teardrops roll down your cheeks, dripping on your beautiful new tutu and making spots on the ribbons woven into the hem. What a waste.

Ribbons?!! Ribbons! You carefully pull two ribbons from your tutu and pin them into your shoe. It's perfect.

You do the same for the other shoe, and just as you finish tying the bow, you hear them call out your name. You dance onto the stage and give the performance of your life. At the end everyone applauds. You feel just like a real fairy princess.

THE END

All the finalists are called onto the stage. You are standing right next to Amy. You're squeezing her hand and she's squeezing yours.

If only you win, you make a silent promise to do everything right from now on. You'll always keep your room neat, do your homework on time, never talk back, and definitely put your toe shoes where they belong. You'll even be nice to your mean, horrible brother. You want to win so much you think you're going to explode.

If only you can win. If only. . . .

Turn to **page 28.**

The director comes out of the audience and climbs onto the stage.

"Thank you all," he says. "I'm sorry there can be only one winner. You were all very good."

Your heart is thumping so loudly you can hardly hear him.

"The winner this year is . . ."

He's looking right in your direction! Or is he looking at Amy?

"Our new fairy princess is . . ."

It's you! You've won!

Everyone rushes up to you. It's the most exciting moment in your life, and it's just the beginning!

THE END

You're going to have to move faster than you ever knew you could. You figure you have about an hour before it will be your turn to perform — an hour to get home, pick up your shoes, and get back to Town Hall.

You run down the subway steps. Lucky for you, you have a token in your pocket, and even luckier, your train is waiting in the station.

You jump on and notice that it's an express. Now you really have a chance, because it's only three stops on the fast train.

Turn to **page 30.**

You reach your stop, dash up the steps, and start running the three blocks to your house. Just then Mrs. Anderson, a friend of your mother's, comes by in her convertible.

"You look like you're in a hurry," she says. "Hop in."

You do, and now you're at your front door. It's only twenty minutes since you left Town Hall.

Go on to the next page.

You race in, grab your shoes, and make it back to the subway. Just as the train pulls up, you hear a woman scream, "Stop that man — he stole my purse!"

Two policemen come running. They have a German shepherd police dog with them. Another dog on the platform begins to bark and howl. Oh, no! The policemen want the conductor to hold up the train until they search every car.

After that record-breaking trip it looks like you're going to be too late. You feel like howling, too.

THE END

You are angry and hurt to think that Gretta could do such an awful thing to you. Amy thinks that Gretta should be reported to the National Ballet Company, and you agree.

When you call to tell them, they are shocked. Their committee calls a meeting for the following day.

After bursting into tears and throwing herself on the floor, Gretta admits what she did. The committee picks her up off the floor and disqualifies her from the contest. Madame Karakov will give you private lessons so you can catch up with the other dancers.

By the time the day of the contest arrives, you feel really prepared. You do your best in the contest, and you come in third. You feel bad that you didn't win, but the next best thing to *you* winning is having your best friend win. Amy is the new fairy princess!

THE END

You go to the lesson anyway, just to make sure it's really true that you're *not* a finalist. And it's a good thing, too, because you are still in the contest. There must have been some kind of mix-up. Boy, were you worried!

Madame Karakov, who coaches the special class, puts you next to Gretta. What rotten luck.

During a very difficult exercise, Gretta whispers to you. Suddenly you realize that Madame Karakov has stopped the lesson.

"That will be enough talking. If you cannot keep quiet for the time you are in this class, you don't belong here. Is that understood, young lady?" says Madame Karakov, staring right at you.

Gretta gives you the sweetest, sugar-coated smile. A few minutes later, Gretta shoves you when no one is looking, and there you are in a *plié* on the floor.

Again, Madame Karakov speaks to you. "Miss, you are disturbing the class."

Turn to **page 34.**

You bite your lip and hold back the tears. Finally the class is over and Madame Karakov announces, "All students are to keep the same place until the contest."

As everyone starts to leave, Madame stops you and tells you to stay after class. Uh oh, Gretta is big trouble for you! Madame Karakov glares at you and says, "If you disrupt the lesson once more, you are out of the class!"

If you ask to be moved away from Gretta, go on to the next page.

If you don't dare say a word to Madame Karakov, turn to **page 53.**

You bite your tongue and tell Madame you are sorry for disturbing the class.

"Fine, my dear, but this cannot happen again."

You know something awful will happen again as long as you're standing next to Gretta. So you have to try another way out.

"Madame Karakov, I'm allergic to perfume, and since Gretta loves to wear it, do you think it's possible to put me next to someone else?" you ask. Madame Karakov replies that she has allergies, too, and she understands your problem.

You'll spend the following weeks working next to a girl named Natasha. She's never been in any of your classes before, but she's a very good dancer. You like her, and you can't help noticing how much she looks like you. In fact, you can hardly believe it.

Turn to **page 36.**

Soon you're friends. It turns out Natasha lives with the strange old lady who sits in the corner during every lesson. Just to see her sit there makes you nervous. You're not sure why. Natasha tells you that the woman is an old friend of her grandmother's. Long ago she was a famous ballerina in Russia. She once danced in cities all over the world.

The week of the contest, Natasha invites you for tea at her house. But the old lady will be there. Do you still want to go?

If you go to tea because you really like Natasha, go on to the next page.

If you go to Natasha's building but change your mind at the last minute, turn to **page 12.**

You are surprised to find that you are having a wonderful time. The old woman tells you stories about her life as a ballerina. There's something magical and mysterious about her. You like her now that you know her better.

The tea tastes strange to you, but the cinnamon cookies are good.

Suddenly, in the middle of all the talk and laughter, you start to sneeze. You can't stop. The woman suggests that you get a handkerchief from her bedroom. It's the second door on the left.

Turn to **page 38.**

You walk through the door then hear the bolt snap. Oh no, the door has closed and you're locked in!

That woman tricked you! She must have put something in the tea to make you sneeze so she could get you into this room.

A flash of light catches your eye and you see something fantastic on the other side of the room. On the floor is what looks like the most beautiful little city. The houses are so small, they could fit in the palm of your hand. A tiny glass window is reflecting the sunlight. There's a bus no bigger than your finger and a street sign that reads LAND OF DANCE.

It's all so pretty that it dazzles you, but you're still very frightened and you start to cry. Tears stream down your face and drip on the ground.

Go on to the next page.

By now you've cried so long that you feel a little dizzy. Then you notice that the houses are not so little anymore, and when you look down the ground is getting closer and closer. You are shrinking! Oh no, it must be that strange tea again.

Now you notice that the teardrops have turned into a salty river — and you're sinking fast. But here comes a boat! It isn't exactly a boat, though. It looks more like a giant floating ballet slipper with lots of people crowded inside.

Turn to **page 40.**

As the boat comes closer, you see that it's filled with dancers. The slipper-boat stops right in front of you. What else is there to do but get inside?

You ride down the river, passing daffodils the size of trees. A sardine as big as a whale swims by and a butterfly glides past like a 747 jet airliner.

Everyone is so nice. You wish you could just relax and enjoy it but you still feel lost. A pretty little girl says hello to you and you ask her where the boat is going.

"We're searching for our lost princess," she tells you.

"Who is she and where did she go?" you ask.

The little girl points to the inside of the boat and says, "See that name written there? That's the lost princess, but we don't know where she is. Everyone in the land is looking for her."

Go on to the next page.

You turn to look where the girl is pointing, and there on the inside of the boat is your name in your own handwriting!

"That's *my* name," you tell her. "I don't understand."

Her eyes light up and she just gapes at you. Everyone stops what they're doing and turns to stare. You feel your cheeks turn bright red, and your ears, too. You're so embarrassed you don't know where to hide.

Turn to **page 42.**

Now a little redheaded boy rushes up and wants to know if that's really your name.

"Sure," you tell him.

"Then that means you're our long-lost princess!"

Everyone on the boat starts jumping up and down, singing with joy.

"We've found our princess!"

You try to act happy, but it's all too much of a shock. While everyone is rejoicing, the captain pulls the boat into a harbor. The news spreads, and within minutes a crowd and a brass band have gathered on the dock to meet you.

Turn to **page 55**

Your stomach feels like you had butterfly soup for lunch. You race to the bus stop just as a bus is approaching. What a lucky break. You hop on. It looks like you might make it. And then — look at all those cars ahead, none of them moving. What a traffic jam! You feel like screaming as you watch the minutes tick by. At last the cars start to move, and then the bus pulls over for no reason.

"What's going on?" you shout at the driver.

"Feels like a flat tire," he answers. "You're going to have to wait for the next bus."

Turn to **page 44.**

And there it is. You jump on, thinking that you still might make the contest. But you're so busy looking at your watch, you don't even realize that the bus is going in the wrong direction.

Your heart feels like it's cracking. Suddenly a gentle hand under your chin lifts your head up. You are nose to nose with the saddest clown-face in the world. You can't help but giggle. That's when you realize that the bus is filled with circus performers.

Turn to **page 51.**

You search through all the garbage — even the smelly stuff. No luck! This is terrible. You know you have a chance to win the contest, but not without your toe shoes. You can still try the laundry room. You cross your fingers, rush back to the house, and dash through the door.

Turn to **page 13.**

You start jumping — little jumps, and then a little bigger and higher, and hey, it's even fun. You're not scared anymore. But boy, do you ever want to push open that door.

Finally your fingertips touch the door, and on the next jump your whole hand touches it, and then with all your strength you push it open.

Your head pops through. "Help!" you yell, as down you go.

Madame Karakov comes running downstairs and lets you out. She lends you new ribbons for your toe shoes. You finally make it onto the stage, and guess what? You're wonderful.

THE END

Good thing you have your library card and bus pass. You reach into your pocket for them, and the two men jump. They take your hands.

"What are you doing?" they growl.

Your voice is trembling as you speak. "I only wanted to show you my identification so I could prove that I'm not who you think I am."

They take a look at your bus pass. "She's not the one," the man next to you says. "Stop the car, let's get rid of her."

You're scared out of your wits, but you keep quiet as the other man says, "What if she tells?"

"Ahh, she's just a kid, no one would believe her anyway." The car stops and they shove you out the door. You run to the nearest phone booth.

If you call Natasha to warn her, go on to the next page.

If you call the police and report what happened, turn to **page 25.**

The line is busy, and you think you're going to go crazy, but finally Natasha answers. You explain the whole story to her, and to your surprise, she's not even scared.

"Don't worry," Natasha says. "This will be our secret. I know they want to get me back, but I'm very well protected. I'll see you at the contest on Friday."

She thanks you for the warning, and tells you that you're a wonderful friend.

If you circle the third word in the last paragraph and the first three letters of the thirteenth word, you will find out how you did at the contest.

THE END

You're wrong. The judges don't think Amy was better. They think she wasn't nearly as good as you, even though she's been taking lessons a year longer. The judges tell you that you were the best dancer they've seen in all the auditions this year. They think you've got a lot of talent, and you'll make a beautiful fairy princess.

THE END

"Wow! Imagine . . . what fun to be in the circus," you whisper to yourself.

As you're looking around the bus you overhear the ringmaster explaining that the show might not go on.

"Katrina, our star ballerina, is sick," he says to someone sitting in a tuxedo suit next to him. "There's no one to replace her for tonight's show," he adds sadly.

You can hardly believe your ears.

"I'm a ballerina," you say, jumping out of your seat. "I can do it."

Your audition consists of several *tour jetés* in the aisle of the bus. Everyone applauds, and you are hired on the spot. You can't wait to tell your parents about your new career . . . circus performer.

THE END

You try to ignore Gretta, but she gets meaner and meaner as the weeks go by.

One day you walk into the bathroom to find your ballet slippers floating in the sink. Gretta really knows how to make someone very unhappy.

Another time, when she thinks you're not looking, she dumps a whole bottle of toe-shoe powder into your ballet bag. This makes you steaming mad!! But you bite your tongue, knowing that the day of the contest is almost here.

Turn to **page 54.**

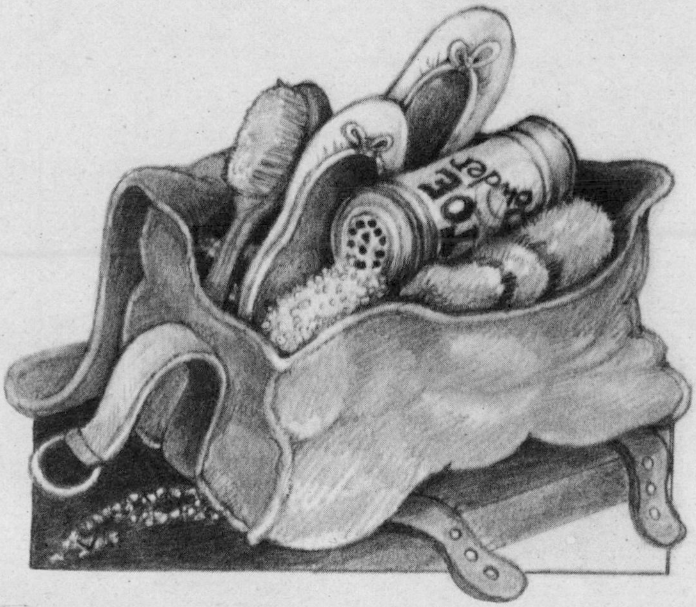

When the big day finally arrives, Gretta's mother is the only one available to drive everyone to Town Hall. She's already five minutes late; now she's ten minutes late. Chances are, she won't even show up. Gretta probably told her mother some kind of story about how you had made other arrangements to get to the contest.

You should have known better! Well, now you've got a big problem and not much time to solve it.

If you decide to look for help from a neighbor, turn to **page 56.**

If you dash out of the house to catch the bus, turn to **page 43.**

The band plays a royal march as you walk down the gangplank. *This isn't too bad,* you think. If only you could have all this attention at home.

But when will you ever see home again? Right now it looks like you are going to spend the rest of your days in this strange world.

Just as you're thinking about home, and missing it, the cheering gets louder. The king and queen are coming! You can't see their faces clearly yet, but something about them looks familiar.

When they finally get close enough to see, you jump up in the air and clap your hands. Who do you think the King and Queen of the Land of Dance are? They are your very own parents!

This is the beginning of a fabulous new life. But it is also . . .

THE END

Just then your brother Harold rides by on his motorbike, and you dash out the door. "Harold, Harold, I need your help!" You don't usually ask him for any favors, because he's always been so mean to you. But after hearing the panic in your voice, he looks very concerned.

He says he'll give you a ride to Town Hall. He gets you there in record time.

You dash into the dressing room, passing Gretta on the way. You get dressed as fast as you can. Now all you have to do is put on your toe shoes, and you're ready to go.

You dig into your ballet bag and pull out the shoes. But as you're about to put them on, you notice that the ribbons that hold the shoes on your feet have been cut off. Oh, no! Gretta again!

If you try to fix them right there, turn to **page 26.**

If you go to the prop room to find some ribbons, go to the next page.

You're digging around in the prop room, turning things upside down. You must move quickly, because you don't want to miss your turn. Then you hear a click at the door. Someone has locked you in! You have a strong feeling you know exactly who it is.

You try the old hanger-in-the-door trick, and that doesn't work.

Then you see a trapdoor in the ceiling. It must open to the stage, right above.

You look all around the room for a ladder or something that will get you close to the trapdoor. Then you notice a little trampoline in the corner of the room. It's your only hope.

You drag the trampoline across so that it's directly below the trapdoor, and jump on top.

Turn to **page 47.**

With horrible smiles, they turn to you and say, "We know who you are, Ms. Natasha Regalinski. We know that you are the most famous young dancer in our country. You thought you could leave our country. You thought you could escape us. Now you know better. We caught you and we are taking you back."

At first you are so surprised and scared you can't even cry. You are in shock! But as you listen you realize there's been a big mistake. You know you *look* a lot like Natasha, but they think you *are* Natasha. You better explain, and fast.

"I am not the person you think I am. I've lived here all my life and I've never been to any other country, and you've made a gigantic mistake."

Turn to **page 48.**